THOMAS & FRIENDS™

May the Best Engine Win!

Illustrated by Tommy Stubbs

A GOLDEN BOOK · NEW YORK

D1302351

Early one morning on the Island of Sodor, Sir Topham Hatt came to the Yard. Thomas and Emily were preparing for a busy day.

Thomas always worked very hard. He was proud to be a Really Useful Engine.

Emily was new. She wanted to prove that she was Really Useful, too. She hoped that Sir Topham Hatt would see how excited she was to start the day.

"Percy is at the Works today," said Sir Topham Hatt. "Thomas, I hope you can help out so that everything gets done on time."

"Why should Thomas get all the work?" asked Emily. "I can do anything he can. I'm faster than him, too!"

Sir Topham Hatt was glad that Emily wanted to help. He told them, "You will still have your own jobs to do. But I can divide up Percy's duties so that both of you will have the same workload today."

Emily knew it would be a long day, but she smiled. She told Thomas, "Now you'll see what I can do."

Thomas was used to long days. "Emily, this might be too much work for you," he teased. "You should let me do more."

"Pfffft!" she puffed. "I'll race you! Whoever finishes and makes it back to the station first is the winner."

"There's enough work for everyone," grumbled Gordon. "Why don't you two get started?"

With a *Peep!* and a *Poop!*, Thomas and Emily left the
station side by side.

Emily's first stop was the Quarry. She'd brought crates full of new tools, and she had to stay in place while the workers unloaded them. After all the crates were taken away, the workers hitched her to freight cars full of large stones.

Emily knew that Really Useful Engines were supposed to be good at waiting. But it was difficult for her to be patient. "Please hurry," she told the workers. "I don't want Thomas to get ahead!"

While Emily was at the Quarry, Thomas was running his Branch Line.

He moved from station to station. At every stop, more passengers got off and Annie and Clarabel got lighter and lighter.

"I'll bet I'm pulling ahead of Emily already," thought Thomas.

Along the way to his last station, Thomas saw Emily. She was going to Suddery with stone from the Quarry. "There you are, slowcoach!" she called.

Thomas laughed. "That stone looks awfully heavy!" he
said.

He hoped that Emily would get tired from hauling such
a heavy load.

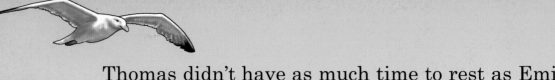

Thomas didn't have as much time to rest as Emily, but he also didn't have to carry as much weight.

His second job was to deliver a load of barrels to the docks. He had to wait for the barrels to be moved onto boats.

Thomas was not a very patient engine, but he knew it would do no good to win the race if he didn't do his job just right.

"The other engines will tease me forever if Emily wins," he thought. He would have to go extra fast to his next stop.

"Is it time to go back to the Shed?" he asked his Driver.

"You still have to haul some Troublesome Trucks to Cronk," said the Driver.

Troublesome Trucks were always bumping and bashing. Thomas had to work hard to keep them in line.

"Don't try anything funny!" he said as they left the station.

But soon Thomas had to stop at a signal.

The Signalman explained, "Some rocks have fallen onto the tracks. You'll have to wait until the way is clear."

"Oh, bother," said Thomas. "I wonder where Emily is now."

Emily had left Suddery. Her final job was a Special along the mountain route.

Along the way, she passed Thomas, who was stopped at the signal.

"Poor Thomas!" she called to him. "Looks like you're stuck!"

Emily sped up.
 She saw a sign warning of a winding track ahead, but she didn't want to slow down and risk losing the race.

The track was difficult, and she was going too fast. Her Driver told her to slow down.

CAUTION
Winding Track
Continue with Care

But it was too late. As Emily took a turn, one of her trucks tipped over!

Now she had to wait for help. "Thomas will get ahead for sure," she thought.

Thomas was having better luck. The rocks had been cleared, and he was almost done with his last job of the day.

He saw Harvey moving on the opposite track. "Hello, Harvey," he peeped. "Where are you headed?"

"Emily's hit a spot of trouble up the line," said Harvey. "Nothing to worry about."

Emily was glad to see Harvey. She thanked him for his help.

"I'll take the rest of the path slowly," she said. "If I'm more careful, I still might beat Thomas."

Thomas was having some difficulty with the Troublesome Trucks. They made him go faster than he wanted to. But his brakes were strong and he was able to stay on the track.

Once the Troublesome Trucks were unhitched, he sped away toward home. "I hope Emily isn't there yet," he thought.

The sun was nearly setting by the time Thomas arrived at the Yard.

He asked Edward whether Emily was already there.

"No," said Edward. "I haven't seen her yet."

Thomas grinned and thought, "I did it! I beat her!"

Emily arrived only a minute later. When she saw Thomas, she frowned. She had really wanted to beat him.

Thomas saw her sad expression. He knew that *he* would have been sad if he had lost, so he decided not to brag.

"That was a close race," he said.

"You won fair and square," said Emily.

"But I'll beat you tomorrow," she added.

Thomas laughed. "We'll see about that!"